Moose, of Course!

Moose, of Course!

written by Lynn Plourde
illustrated by Jim Sollers

DOWN EAST BOOKS ROCKPORT · MAINE

With love to my "moose child," Lucas. —L. P.

This is for Jillie. —J. S.

Text copyright © 1999 by Lynn Plourde

Illustrations copyright © 1999 by James Thomas Sollers IV

ISBN 0-89272-454-4 hardcover • 0-89272-473-0 paperback

Production assistance by Lurelle Cheverie

Color separations, printing, and binding by
Oceanic Graphic Printing Productions Ltd.

Printed in Hong Kong

2 4 6 8 9 7 5 3 1

Down East Books
ROCKPORT • MAINE

Orders: 1-800-766-1670

LIBRARY OF CONGRESS CATALOGING-IN-PUBLICATION DATA

Plourde, Lynn, 1955–
    Moose, of course / Lynn Plourde ; pictures by Jim Sollers.
      p.   cm.
    SUMMARY: A persistent young boy tries everything he can think of to attract a moose, but it isn't until he is forced to "do nuthin" that he is successful.
    ISBN 0-89272-454-4 (hc.)
    ISBN 0-89272-473-0 (pb.)
    [1. Moose Fiction.   2. Patience Fiction.   3. Stories in rhyme.]   I. Sollers, Jim, 1951– ill. II. Title.
PZ8.3.P5586922 Mo 1999
[E]--dc21
                                 99-27492
                                    CIP

There was a boy
who headed north.
Wanted to see moose,
of course.

He rode a bicycle
built for deuce,
in hopes of sharing it
with a moose.

He honked his horn
and yelled, "Here, moose!"
What joined him instead
was a pedaling goose.

Bonkity-bonk—A bike built for deuce.
Honkity-honk—A pedaling goose.

The boy stopped at
a sporting-goods store
and asked for a bottle
of their best moose lure.

A worker there
just shook his head.
Suggested the boy
"do nuthin" instead.

"Do nuthin!" he cried,
"That'll serve no use.
If I can't buy a lure,
then I'll be a girl moose!"

He dressed himself up
in some stilts and a hide,
added some lipstick,
then sashayed outside.

He batted his lashes,
gave a big "AROOOO!"
But all he heard back
was a mighty "MOOOO!"

Bonkity-bonk—A bike built for deuce.
Honkity-honk—A pedaling goose.
Arooooity-roooo—A boy who sashayed.
Mooooity-moooo—A bull who was swayed.

Into a pet shop
the boy stopped for feed,
to buy pond fronds—
a favorite moose weed.

The pet shop owner
shook her head,
suggested the boy
"do nuthin" instead.

"Do nuthin!" he cried,
"No way! I can't.
If you don't sell moose weeds,
then I'll find my own plants."

He picked and gathered
some greenish weeds,
then wrapped himself up
from his nose to his knees.

Holding his breath,
he took a dip.
But fish, not moose,
started to nip.

Bonkity-bonk—A bike built for deuce.
Honkity-honk—A pedaling goose.
Arooooity-roooo—A boy who sashayed.
Mooooity-moooo—A bull who was swayed.
Glubity-glub—A boy who dipped.
Nibblity-nub—A fish who nipped.

At a hardware store
the boy asked for a noose,
one rugged enough
to catch a big moose.

SPEC
2 FO

But that store clerk
just shook his head.
Suggested the boy
"do nuthin" instead.

"Do nuthin!" he cried,
"Never! You'll see—
I'll make my own trap.
The moose won't go free."

He spliced and he knotted
his gigantic snare.
Beware the moose
who stepped in there.

But he triggered the trap
with his own big toe.
The snare went *whoosh!*
and he yelled, "WHOA!"

Bonkity-bonk—A bike built for deuce.

Honkity-honk—A pedaling goose.

Arooooity-roooo—A boy who sashayed.

Mooooity-moooo—A bull who was swayed.

Glubity-glub—A boy who dipped.

Nibblity-nub—A fish who nipped.

Bangity-bop—A gigantic snare.

Whooshity-whop—A boy in the air.

So, there the boy
hung from the tree.
Couldn't get down.
Couldn't get free.

Upside-down,
he shook his head
and muttered,
"I'll do nuthin' instead."

A little lull.
A pause, a stare,
a gaze, a gawk. . .
Look! What's there?

A whole family of moose—
a bull, calf, and cow—
moseyed on out.
The boy shouted, "Wow!"

Bonkity-bonk—A bike built for deuce.
Honkity-honk—A pedaling goose.
Arooooity-roooo—A boy who sashayed.
Mooooity-moooo—A bull who was swayed.
Glubity-glub—A boy who dipped.
Nibblity-nub—A fish who nipped.
Bangity-bop—A gigantic snare.
Whooshity-whop—A boy in the air.
Pausity-pause—A bull, calf, and cow.
Gawkity-gawz—A wonderous wow.

Yes, there was a boy
who headed north.
He finally *did* see moose,
of course!

THE END